THE TREASURE CHEST

To my editor, Margery Cuyler, and my family—David, Vicky, Daniel, and Agnes—for their support over the years.
—R.W.

For Margery, Danielle, and all who make room in their lives for small acts of selfless kindness.
—W.H.

THE TREASURE CHEST

A Chinese Tale

retold by Rosalind C. Wang

illustrated by Will Hillenbrand

Holiday House/New York

Once upon a time in southern China, a poor widow lived with her son, Laifu, in a small cottage near the sea. The only valuable thing they owned was an old fishing net. Every morning at sunrise, Laifu would catch fish to sell later at the market. Then he would collect firewood for his mother before going to work in the fields.

Not far from the cottage lived a beautiful orphan girl named Pearl. Her skin was as smooth as ivory. Her long hair shone like black silk. Her eyes were as bright as morning stars. Whenever Laifu finished his daily chores, he would play with Pearl. As they grew older, Laifu and Pearl fell deeply in love. They soon planned to get married.

One afternoon, when Laifu was returning home from the market, he saw a rainbow-colored fish caught between two rocks along the seashore. The fish could hardly breathe and could only wiggle its tail.

"What a beautiful big fish!" said Laifu to himself. "I can sell it for much money." But the fish looked sadly at him. Its mouth opened and closed as if trying to tell him something. When Laifu saw its suffering, he scooped the fish up, put it back into the water, and watched it swim away. Then he continued his journey home.

Now, near Laifu's village, there lived an evil ruler named Funtong. He was always cheating people and stealing the hardworking peasants' crops and cattle. He let nothing stand in his way. Although no one respected him, everyone obeyed him because he controlled thousands of soldiers.

One day, Funtong traveled through the village and saw Pearl hanging out clothes to dry. He was stunned by her beauty.

When he found out she was engaged to a young fisherman, he offered to trade one thousand gold pieces for the beautiful girl. Laifu firmly rejected his proposal. This made Funtong furious. No one had ever dared to refuse him!

Funtong realized he could not kidnap Pearl. If he did, the villagers would become angry and turn against him. Since he knew that village people admired heroes, he challenged Laifu to a contest. If Laifu lost, Funtong would become a hero and marry Pearl.

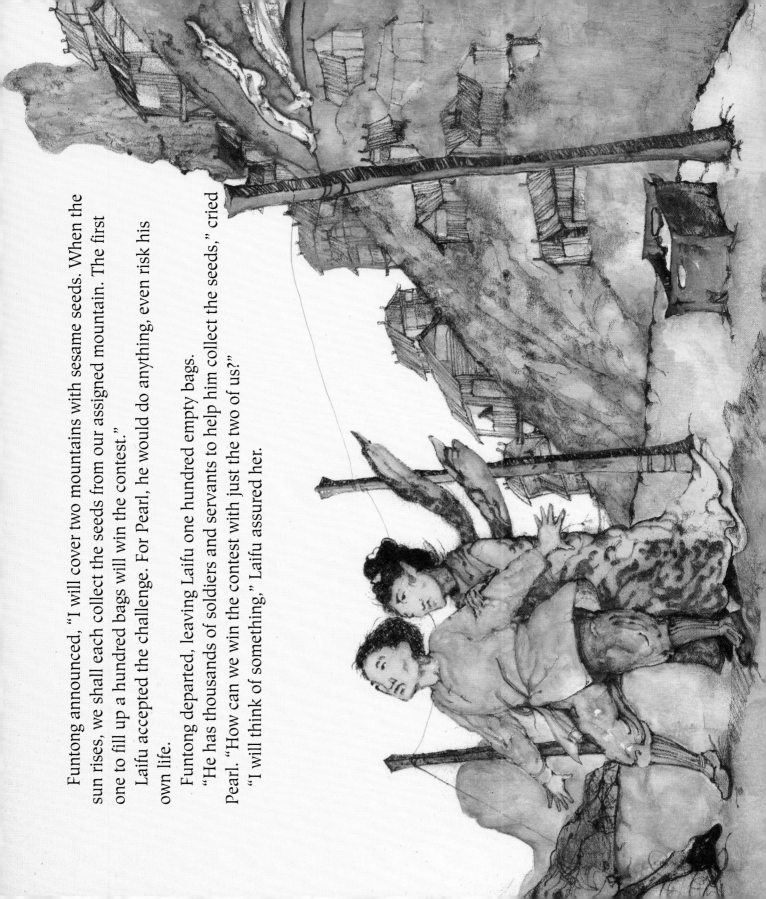

Funtong announced, "I will cover two mountains with sesame seeds. When the sun rises, we shall each collect the seeds from our assigned mountain. The first one to fill up a hundred bags will win the contest."

Laifu accepted the challenge. For Pearl, he would do anything, even risk his own life.

Funtong departed, leaving Laifu one hundred empty bags.

"He has thousands of soldiers and servants to help him collect the seeds," cried Pearl. "How can we win the contest with just the two of us?"

"I will think of something," Laifu assured her.

Later that night, as Laifu tossed on his bed, he heard someone calling "Laifu . . . Laifu . . ." in a soft, sweet voice. When he looked outside, he saw a big turtle next to his window.

"Do not be afraid. I am the messenger from the Ocean Palace," the turtle said. "Remember the rainbow-colored fish you once saved? That fish is the son of the Ocean King. He changes from boy to fish when he swims back and forth to the underwater Palace. The King has heard about your contest with Funtong and wishes to see you. Please come with me. I will take you to the Ocean King's Palace."

Laifu followed the turtle to the seashore. He climbed on its back and closed his eyes as it jumped into the sea. Laifu heard water splashing around him, but somehow he did not get wet.

When the turtle told him to open his eyes, he found himself in a beautiful palace, where he saw the Ocean King seated on a seashell throne. Behind the King stood a young boy clad in a rainbow-colored robe. Laifu knew at once that the boy was the fish he had saved.

"Thank you for saving my son," said the Ocean King. "Now I want to help you."

"But your Majesty," Laifu answered, "I only did what I thought was right."

"Laifu, I owe my life to you," said the Ocean King's son.

The king handed Laifu a small wooden box with three bamboo sticks in it. "Whenever you are in great danger, break one of these sticks."

"Thank you, your Majesty. I am grateful for your kindness." Laifu accepted the box and put it in his pocket.

"Now, Turtle will take you home," said the Ocean King. "Soon the sun will rise and Funtong will be there. Good luck to you!"

Laifu climbed on Turtle's back and was quickly whisked back to the seashore. As soon as Laifu arrived home, he ran to tell Pearl what had happened. When the sun began to rise, they broke the first bamboo stick. A giant monk appeared, surrounded by a red cloud of smoke. "What can I do for you, Master?" the monk asked.

After Laifu described the contest, the monk handed him a bird cage and said, "When Funtong appears, open the cage." Then the giant monk disappeared in a gust of wind.

An hour later, Funtong arrived with thousands of soldiers and servants to collect the sesame seeds.

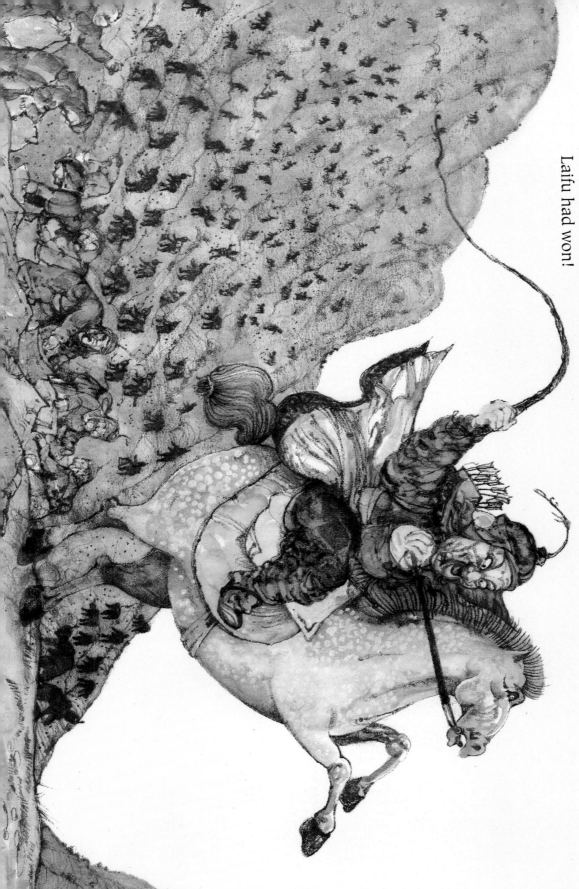

"Aha!" laughed Funtong. "Only two of you? I will surely be the winner!" He whipped his servants to speedily pick up sesame seeds.

Quietly, Laifu opened the bird cage. Thousands of sparrows flew out and searched for the tiny seeds. In only a few moments, they filled one hundred bags. Laifu had won!

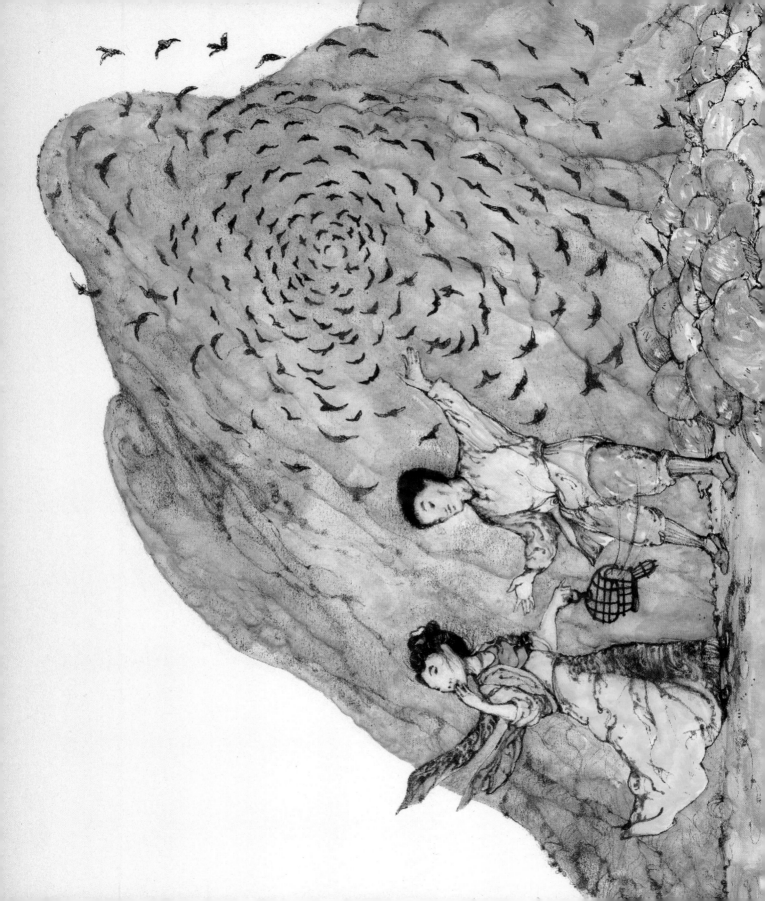

Funtong was furious. "This contest is not fair," he shouted. "I insist on holding another one. Let us have a horse race. Whoever first reaches the peak of that snow-covered mountain will win the beautiful Pearl."

Pearl worried about the second contest. "Funtong has thousands of excellent horses in his stable," she said to Laifu. "We don't even have one. How can we win the race?"

"Have no fear," Laifu said.

Together they broke the second bamboo stick. After a cloud of green smoke cleared, a different giant monk bowed to Laifu and said, "What can I do for you, Master?"

When Laifu told him about the race, the monk answered, "You will find a horse in your yard. Ride the horse and you will see what happens!" Then he disappeared in another gust of wind.

Laifu went to his yard and saw a skinny horse looking for food. He fed the animal before he went to bed.

The next morning, Funtong arrived on a strong horse with a bright golden saddle. When he saw Laifu's skinny horse, he laughed until he almost choked.

"Laifu," he shouted, "where did you get this little donkey? Be careful, you might crush it! Ha, Ha, Ha!"

As the seashell horn sounded to start the race, Funtong's horse shot forward like an arrow, leaving a thick cloud of dust and Laifu behind.

When Funtong had almost reached the foot of the mountain, Laifu patted the skinny horse. "Come on, my good horse, we can't let that evil Funtong win our beautiful Pearl!"

Like a flash of lightning, both the horse and Laifu landed on top of the mountain. Funtong was dumbfounded to see them there when he arrived.

"This is impossible!" he fumed.

Once again, Funtong's pride was hurt. He insisted on a third contest. "Whoever can first crush this rocky hill will win Pearl," said the evil ruler.

"Funtong has hundreds of spades and shovels," cried Pearl, "and thousands of servants to use them. What shall we do?"

"Don't worry," Laifu again comforted Pearl, "let us break our last bamboo stick."

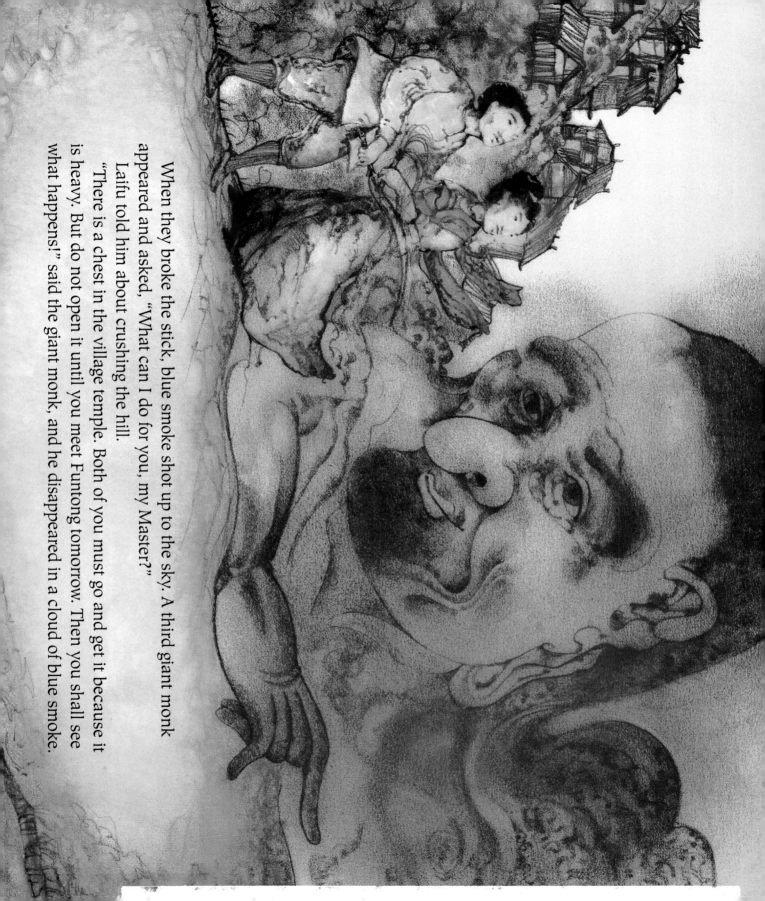

When they broke the stick, blue smoke shot up to the sky. A third giant monk appeared and asked, "What can I do for you, my Master?"

Laifu told him about crushing the hill.

"There is a chest in the village temple. Both of you must go and get it because it is heavy. But do not open it until you meet Funtong tomorrow. Then you shall see what happens!" said the giant monk, and he disappeared in a cloud of blue smoke.

Laifu and Pearl found the chest, but while they were trying to move it, they heard strange noises. "What's in there?" asked Laifu. He started to open it.

"Oh, no," Pearl cried, pulling Laifu's hands away from the chest. "Remember what the monk told us? You must obey him."

Reluctantly Laifu agreed. As they carried the chest home, the strange noises continued. Laifu was greatly tempted to find out what was inside. Once again, he tried to persuade Pearl to let him peek into the chest. Then he heard a loud voice saying, "Do not open the chest! Just carry it home."

Laifu recognized the voice. He quickly pulled his hand away and said to Pearl, "It is Turtle who took me to the Ocean Palace. I must not open it."

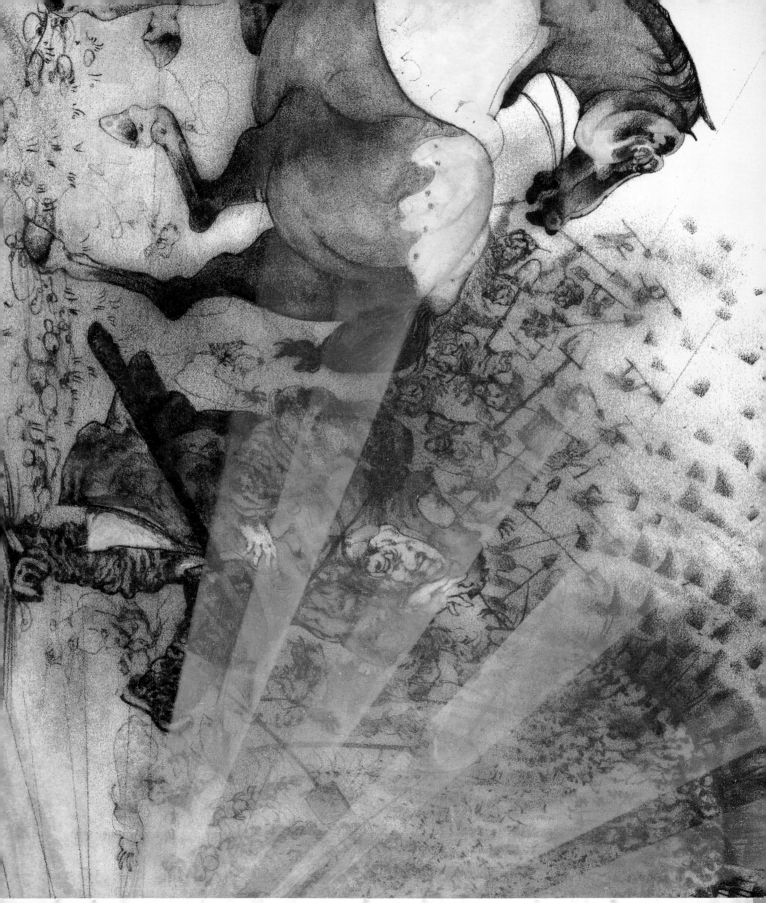

Before the sun rose, Funtong brought thousands of soldiers and servants to the village.

"Are you ready for the contest, Laifu?" he yelled. "Why don't you just give in? There is no way that you can crush that hill!"

"Funtong, I accept your challenge and I will win," cried Laifu.

Then Laifu and Pearl opened the chest. Thousands of toy soldiers, carrying all kinds of weapons, started climbing out of the chest.

"Master!" they shouted, "what do you want us to do?"

Pointing at the rocky hill, Laifu and Pearl said, "Please crush it!"

The tiny soldiers marched up and leveled the hill into small pieces. Then they returned and stood in front of the chest.

Once again, Funtong was surprised and angry.

"There will be no more contests!" he shouted. Funtong ordered his soldiers to kidnap Pearl.

But as Funtong and his soldiers approached the cottage, Laifu and Pearl pointed their fingers toward the evil ruler. At once, the toy soldiers marched forward bravely. Using their tiny weapons, they defeated Funtong and his entire army.

With feasting and dancing, the villagers celebrated their victory and the marriage of Laifu and Pearl. Even the Ocean King's son and Turtle joined them. Peace returned to the little seashore village. Never again did the people have to worry about the evil Funtong.

Author's Note When I was a little girl, my parents entertained me with songs and stories from different countries. One of my favorite Chinese tales was "The Treasure Chest." Neither my parents nor I can pinpoint exactly when and where the story took place. We have not been able to find it in a printed format. Also, the story probably kept changing as it was retold by generations of storytellers. In my retelling of "The Treasure Chest," I have tried to remain faithful to the oral version I heard from my parents.

—*Rosalind C. Wang*

Illustrator's Note Chinese folklore expresses ancient concepts of the natural and magical world. Often these worlds are filled with supernatural characters—rainbow-colored fish, turtles, monks, magic animals, and so on. The costumes and setting in the illustrations for "The Treasure Chest" were roughly taken from the introspection and lyricism of southern Sung paintings (A.D. 1200).

—*Will Hillenbrand*

Text copyright © 1995 by Rosalind C. Wang
Illustrations copyright © 1995 by Will Hillenbrand
All rights reserved
Printed in the United States of America
First Edition

Library of Congress Cataloging-in-Publication Data
Wang, Rosalind C.
The treasure chest: a Chinese tale/retold by Rosalind C. Wang;
illustrated by Will Hillenbrand.—1st. ed.
p.   cm.
Summary: A rainbow-colored magic fish helps Laifu protect his
bride-to-be from the evil ruler Funtong.
ISBN 0-8234-1114-1
[1. Fairy tales.   2. Folklore—China.]   I. Hillenbrand, Will,
ill. II. Title.
PZ8.W1812th   1995   93-20744   CIP
398.2—dc20   AC
[E]